MUDDY PAWS

Coaching Madcap

The Muddy Paws series

1. Coaching Madcap

2. Making Friends with Breezy

3. Rocking with Roxy and Rosie

4. Saving Snowdrop

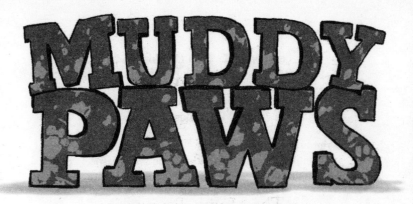

MUDDY PAWS

Coaching
Madcap

JENNY OLDFIELD

Illustrated by Paul Howard

Hodder
Children's
Books

A division of Hachette Children's Books

Text copyright © Jenny Oldfield, 2013
Illustrations copyright © Paul Howard, 2013

First published in Great Britain in 2013
by Hodder Children's Books

1

A Catalogue record for this book is available
from the British Library

ISBN 978 1 444 91318 7

Hodder Children's Books
A division of Hachette Children's Books
Hachette UK Limited
338 Euston Road,
London NW1 3BH
www.hachette.co.uk

To Lola, Jude
and Evan –
my little stars!
JO

Chapter One

The path to the beach ran along the edge of the cliff to wooden steps that led down to wide open sands.

"Ouch!" Lexi cried as she chased Alfie through some prickly gorse bushes.

"Wait for me," Lily yelled as Lexi and Alfie charged ahead. She looked down at white waves breaking on the shore and up at a perfect blue sky.

Lexi didn't listen. She dashed after her mixture-of-all-sorts pup until they reached the golden sand. Then she kicked off her

1

shoes and ran after Alfie into the sea. Waves lapped at her ankles.

"It's c-c-cold!" she wailed.

Lily took her time. She crossed the warm sand then dipped her toe into the water, stooping to pick up a white shell. Alfie dashed past, splashing her from head to toe.

"Hey!" she cried.

"Sorry," Lexi said, the corners of her mouth twitching.

"No you're not."

"You're right – I'm not." Lexi grinned at Lily then burst out laughing.

So Lily splashed spray at her cousin. Lexi splashed back and soon they were both drenched. Meanwhile, Alfie charged along the water's edge.

Lily looked up. "Where's he off to?" she wondered aloud.

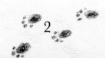

"He's found someone to play with."

In the distance Lexi spotted a group of four people with a small Jack Russell.

"Who are they?" Lily asked.

"I don't know. I've never seen them on the beach before."

Quickly Lexi and Lily ran after Alfie and caught up with him.

The Jack Russell split from his young owners and came bounding up. He raced in circles around the girls then jumped high in the air. *Yip-yap, yip-yip!*

"Down, Madcap!" a voice called.

Alfie wagged his tail and looked on.

Yip! Like a mini-hurricane, Madcap charged past. He raced to the water's edge then whirled around and rampaged back.

Yip-yip! Bounce-bounce.

"Madcap, come here!"

The group of boys drew close to Lexi and Lily. They were dressed in identical T-shirts and jeans. One came forward to try to grab his naughty pup.

"Oh!" Lily gasped and her mouth fell open.

"Wow!" Lexi murmured. Like Lily, she recognized the dog walkers.

"It's . . ." Lily hissed out of the corner of her mouth.

"I know!" For once Lexi was speechless.

There was no doubt in either of their minds. They'd just bumped into Luke, Ryan, Jude and Sammy. In other words, the four members of Up Front – only the most famous boy band in the country.

Yip! Madcap jumped on Alfie and wrestled him.

"What do we do?" Lexi muttered. She

4

was one of the band's biggest fans – at her home just outside Mellingham she had a giant Up Front poster pinned to her bedroom wall. But coming face to face with pop star royalty she was suddenly shy.

"Grab Alfie?" Lily suggested.

But it was already too late. By now Alfie was chasing Madcap into the waves, making paw prints in the smooth wet sand.

"Alfie, come!" Lexi called.

Slowly Alfie left off playing and came back. He bounded up, then shook himself dry, showering Lily with salty water. Madcap chased after him.

"Sit," Lexi told Alfie.

Alfie sat and cocked his head to one side. One of his ears was pricked, the other flopped. His black and white fur was drenched, his pink tongue hung out.

"Down, Madcap!" Luke cried as the Jack Russell scampered back. "Sit!"

But Madcap leaped and yapped. He hurled himself at Lexi, then at Lily. He ran circles around them.

Luke blushed. "Whoa, sorry about that," he mumbled. "Madcap, stay down!"

"It's OK," Lily told him. Luke was wearing an Up Front T-shirt, his feet were bare, his jeans rolled halfway up his calves and his fair hair flopped forward into his blue eyes.

"Hey, Luke, we're out of here," one of the other boys told him. It was Jude – the cutest of all the band, the one with the cheeky grin that all the girls loved.

"See you later," Sammy and Ryan agreed. And all three strolled on towards the wooden steps.

Luke nodded. "Sit!" he told Madcap as sternly as he could.

Yip-yip! The bundle of brown and white energy took no notice. He wagged his pointed tail and pounced at Alfie, inviting him to play again.

But this time Alfie stayed at Lexi's feet. *Sorry, not allowed.*

Luke sighed and turned to her. "How did you train your dog to do as he's told?"

"I took him to classes in Mellingham."

"So how old was he when you did that?" Luke asked as he watched Madcap pounce, twirl, run and roll in the wet sand.

"I got Alfie from the rescue centre when he was twelve weeks old but we waited until he was about six months before we started," Lexi recalled. "He's super smart so it didn't take long."

"Madcap's ten months old now. And he's smart too." Luke frowned. "You'd never believe it, but Jack Russells are known for being able to learn lots of tricks. They even star in major films and TV shows."

Lily laughed as Madcap began to dig. He scooped up sand with his front paws until there was a hole deep enough for him to jump into – *splash*, straight into the pool that had quickly formed. The pup crawled out with a bewildered look.

"Actually, it should be fairly easy to coach Madcap if you took him to the right classes," Lexi told Luke.

"The problem is, I'm away from home a lot," Luke sighed. "I'm always touring with the band or recording in the studio. And Mum and Dad both work so they don't have time to train him properly either."

"Hmmm." Lexi glanced at Lily to see if she was thinking the same thing.

Lily raised her eyebrows. Her grey eyes sparkled but she said nothing.

For a while there was silence as Alfie sat obediently and Madcap jumped up in the air, up-down, up-down, as if on a trampoline.

"The thing is . . .' Luke spoke slowly and looked straight at Lexi and Lily with his bright blue eyes. "I've gone and done something pretty dumb."

9

The girls held their breath and waited for more.

"You know the county show they hold in Mellingham at the beginning of June?"

Lily nodded. "The one where they have sheep and cows and all different kinds of animals?"

"That's the one."

Lily and Lexi waited for Luke to scold Madcap, who had pounced on the frayed hem of his jeans.

"You'll never guess what I did – I promised the show organizer I'd make an appearance."

"Wow!" Lexi said.

"Cool!" Lily sighed. A personal appearance by Luke from Up Front would definitely pull in the crowds.

"No, not cool," Luke argued, running a

hand through his floppy hair while Madcap chewed his jeans. "I also promised to take Madcap along with me."

"So?" Lily and Lexi asked.

"You don't understand," Luke groaned.

Madcap growled and chewed.

Finally his owner picked him up. An overjoyed Madcap licked Luke's face. "I promised to enter him into the dog agility trials."

"Oh." Lily got it. To enter the Mellingham Show, Madcap would have to learn how to do tricks in front of the judges.

"Does he have to jump fences and run through tunnels?" Lexi asked eagerly.

"Yep." Luke tickled Madcap's tummy then set him down on the sand. He stood back and watched him scamper towards the sea.

Lexi and Lily waited a split second then they both spoke at once. "We'll do it!" they gushed. "Please, Luke – let us train Madcap for the Mellingham Show!"

Chapter Two

"Hey, crazy girls – time to begin!" Luke said when he dropped Madcap off at Sea View Café the next morning.

Sea View was where Lily lived with her mum and dad. Lexi was staying there while her dad worked abroad.

"Why are we crazy?" Lily wanted to know.

"Because you want to train my crazy dog – that means you must be mad too."

"But we already *love* Madcap!" Lexi and Lily protested.

"My point exactly," Luke said with a grin. "And I'll tell you what – if you teach Madcap agility tricks, I promise to give you a present in return."

"What? What?" Lexi and Lily clamoured.

Luke thought for a while. "How about two copies of our next CD?"

"Yes! Yes!" they cried.

"And . . . two Up Front T-shirts, signed by all four of us."

"Excellent!" Lily sighed, while Lexi was lost for words again.

Luke had to go straight up to London with the band, he told the girls. "So can you please take Madcap back to my parents' house on the green after the session?"

"Will do!" Lexi promised, lifting Madcap up and waving his front paw. "Bye!"

"So!" Lily said eagerly as soon as she, Lexi, Alfie and Madcap were left alone on the lawn which linked the house with her mum's café. "Let's make a start. First we have to teach Madcap how to sit."

Lily took out a bag of treats to give to Luke's puppy whenever he did something right. She showed it to Lexi. "It said on the website that we have to reward good behaviour."

"Which website?" Lexi was too busy putting Madcap down on the grass and chasing after him to pay much attention. She watched him make a beeline for her Aunty Jo's flower bed. "Sto-o-o-p!" she yelled.

"The 'Training Jack Russell Pups' site that I found last night," Lily replied. It had told her how to teach the first two commands: "Sit!" and "Down!"

"Stop!" Lexi called again. Madcap had made a mad dash into the middle of the flowers and was digging up some bright red tulips. "Alfie, help!"

Cocking his head to one side, Alfie thought for a while. Their cheeky visitor was busily destroying the garden. OK, so it had been fun playing with Madcap on the beach yesterday, but did he really want to get his paws dirty by dragging the little pest out of the flower bed?

"Alfie, do something!" Lexi begged, racing across the lawn and throwing herself headlong. She reached for the naughty pup, but just as she got her hands around the

17

rascal's tummy, he broke free and headed straight for the entrance to the café.

Here we go! At last Alfie decided to rush to the rescue. He sprinted to cut Madcap off, ears flapping. He crouched low like a sheepdog herding sheep. When Madcap saw him blocking his path, he stopped dead and whimpered.

"Good boy, Alfie!" Lily called. She and Lexi crept up on Madcap from behind.

"Phew – got you!" Lexi cried as she lunged forward.

He wriggled and squirmed but this time Lexi held him tight.

"Now," Lily said, taking out the pages which she'd printed off from the website. They contained ten hot tips for training your Jack Russell. "Let's start with teaching you to sit."

* * *

Lexi set Madcap down on the grass. "Sit!" she said.

He stood firm and wagged his tail, gazing up at Lily with his adorable brown eyes.

For the tenth time Lily held a dog biscuit in front of his nose. "Sit!" she repeated as she moved the biscuit up and backwards over the top of his head, just like the website told her to do. The method was meant to make him lean back his head, lower his hindquarters and sit down at the same time. Then she could praise him and slip him his treat.

But no. Madcap leaned his head back, gave a yip then went into a quick sideways roll. He sprang up and started to yap and jump, chasing his tail, rolling and jumping again. Up-down, up-down on his invisible trampoline.

"Sit!" Lexi said.

"Down, boy!" Lily used a stern voice. This time she had to hold the biscuit in front of his nose then slowly lower it to the ground.

The website told her that Madcap would follow the biscuit with his nose.

"Down!" Lexi copied Lily's strict tone.

Madcap sniffed the treat as he lowered his head until it rested on the grass.

"He did it!" Lexi cried. "Good boy! Give him the biscuit, Lily – he actually did it."

But no again. Madcap didn't wait for Lily to give him his reward – he just darted his head forward and snatched the treat from between her fingers.

"Ouch!" she said. Madcap's teeth were pin sharp.

* * *

"Come!" Lexi called across the lawn.

Alfie lay at her side, looking bored. Did

Lexi and Lily really think any of this was going to work?

Lily stood with Madcap by the wrecked flower bed. She held him back with both hands. "Have you got the biscuit ready?" she asked Lexi.

Lexi held it up then repeated the command. "Come, Madcap, come!"

"Ready – go!" Lily said, releasing him on cue.

"Come!" Lexi called.

Yip-yap-yap! Oh the joy of running free, of jumping and rolling, digging and racing on. Who cared about a biscuit treat when you had a whole garden to play in?

Lily and Lexi watched in dismay as Madcap scampered between two holly bushes, plunged into the goldfish pond, jumped out soaking wet and dashed through

the tulip bed before disappearing into the tea shop.

Nightmare!

"Shoo!" After ten seconds Lily's mum appeared in the doorway. She was using a broom to try and sweep muddy Madcap out of her café.

The puppy darted between her legs and scooted back inside.

"Uh-oh." Lily felt her stomach tie up in knots. Her mum was proud of her clean floors and pretty table cloths, of her round tables with their china teacups, tinkling silver spoons and vases of flowers.

"Shoo!" Jo chased Madcap out of the café and into the tiny gift shop that led out to the car park.

"Let's grab him," Lexi said. She was the first to run across the lawn, around the side of the building to meet Madcap as he fled from her Aunty Jo.

Lily and Alfie followed hard on her heels.

"No dogs allowed!" Jo cried, sweeping Madcap out of the gift shop into Lexi's arms.

Yip! Madcap jumped up, wriggled with joy and licked Lexi's face.

But Lily's heart sank when she saw her mum's angry frown.

"Lily, come in here," she said.

Lily went into the gift shop. She saw that Madcap had knocked over a display of greetings cards and overturned a box containing "Welcome to Devon" badges.

"And in here," Jo said sternly, leading Lily into the café.

Lily groaned. Madcap had upset her mum's customers. A small boy was crying on his mother's lap, an older man shook his head, and a woman in a cycling helmet scraped her upturned scone off the tablecloth.

"Look!" Jo pointed at the trail of muddy paw prints that Madcap had left. "All over my nice clean floor!"

Chapter Three

"Training a puppy is not as easy as it looks," Lily admitted to Luke's mum.

She and Lexi had taken Madcap home to Beech House on the Green. He'd dragged them all the way there on the lead.

"He doesn't understand 'Heel!'" Lexi explained. *Or "Sit!" or "Down!" or "Come!"* she thought.

"Oh dear, has he been a naughty boy?" Mrs Walker sighed as she took Madcap and tucked him under her arm. "Has Luke's puppy put you off dog training for life?"

"No way!" Lexi insisted. "We'll call for him again tomorrow."

"Bye, Madcap," Lily said, giving his head a pat.

Yip! he said.

"Be good," Lexi added.

"Fat chance of that," Mrs Walker sighed as she closed the front door.

* * *

"We haven't been put off, have we?" Lexi checked with Lily as they walked back to Sea View.

"No, but—"

"It's your mum," Lexi interrupted. "She doesn't want Madcap anywhere near her tea shop, and I don't really blame her."

Lily nodded. "So we have to train him somewhere else – not on the lawn."

"Hmm – how about the empty paddock

at the bottom of your garden?"

"Good idea." Lily pictured the small field which the family owned. It was scattered with buttercups and daisies and overlooked the cliff. A tall hedge bordered it on all sides. There was a gate that could be kept safely shut.

"Let's do it!" Lexi declared.

"Dad, can you put on your Facebook page that we're training Luke Walker's puppy for the Mellingham Show?" Lily asked after lunch. "Luke's fans will think it's cool."

Matt was working at his computer on the mail-order business for speciality teas that he ran from home.

"Luke Walker, the pop star," Lexi prompted. "Uncle Matt, this is mega news!"

"Luke Walker, the lead singer with Up

Front," Lily reminded him. "Come on, Dad – you know who they are!"

"Yes, but I can't put it on Facebook without asking your mum," Matt decided. "Not after what happened this morning."

"She'll be fine." Lily was sure that her mum would agree to their training plan once they'd explained about using the paddock.

"Alfie's going to help," Lexi told him. "I'll get him to show Madcap how to sit and stay. Alfie's really good at it, aren't you, Alfie?"

Alfie came and snuggled up beside Lexi on the sofa – his favourite position. He wagged his tail gently to and fro.

"Remember those muddy paws all over your mum's clean floor," Matt reminded Lily.

"But we're not going to give in after one session." Lily was prepared to work hard, taking more facts from the website and doing everything they could to teach Madcap to do agility tricks and get him ready for the county show.

"Uncle Matt, we know Madcap's not exactly well-behaved," Lexi argued. "That's because he's young. But he's totally cute and gorgeous and we love him."

"Yeah, he's cute," Matt agreed. "And I

have to admit, Lexi, that you've done a good job with Alfie."

Alfie wagged his tail harder at the mention of his name.

"We know we'll have to go back to basics," Lily told him. "Tomorrow we'll do 'Sit!' and 'Down!' again. The day after we'll move on to 'Come!' and 'Fetch!' and 'Heel!'"

"Very organized." Matt liked this about his daughter – she was sensible and you could always rely on her to do what she promised. Lexi was different though – much more scatterbrained. You could tell that by the way she kicked off her shoes and left them lying in the middle of the floor, the way she often forgot to run a comb through her dark, curly hair.

"Hey!" Lexi said, suddenly jumping up from the sofa.

"What now?" Matt asked.

"Lily, come outside – I've just had a brilliant idea!"

* * *

"*Lots* of people are like Luke," Lexi told Lily as they stood ankle-deep in daisies and buttercups, looking out across the paddock towards the sea. "They have problems with their pets."

"So what?" Lily didn't understand what Lexi was getting at. She pulled a stick from under the hedge and threw it for Alfie to fetch.

"The owners don't have the time to deal with it, but we're on half-term holiday so we do."

"Yeah – we have two whole weeks, which is why we're helping Luke with Madcap."

"Exactly! But what about us helping other

people too? Say if there was an old lady with a cat and she couldn't stop him from scratching her furniture, or a girl with a pony that spooked, or a farmer with an orphan lamb…"

"Whoa!" Lily said. "Are you saying we – you and me – could deal with stuff like that?"

"Why not? I'm crazy about animals, so are you."

Alfie came running back with the stick. Lily threw it again. "And we do have this empty paddock to work in," she said slowly.

"We could help *everyone*!" Lexi's thoughts raced on. "Kids with hamsters who run away, someone with a pet rabbit that won't eat lettuce."

Lily warmed to the idea. "We could look it all up on the internet."

"We could give ourselves a name and set

up a website – your dad would help."

"What would the name be?" Lily wondered aloud.

"Pet Problem Solvers? Claws and Paws? Furry Friends?" These were the first names that flew into Lexi's head.

Lily didn't like any of them. She remembered the trail of dirt from the flower bed that Madcap had left on the tea shop floor. "Let's call ourselves Muddy Paws," she decided. "We can design a logo and have it printed on T-shirts. Let's advertise and say there's no pet problem too big or too small for us to solve!"

Chapter Four

"Muddy Paws – I like the name," Lily's dad said with a slow smile.

It was late afternoon, the café was closed and Jo was upstairs changing into her running kit, getting ready to go for a run along the cliff path. She came down into the kitchen with her long dark hair tied up in a ponytail, ready to fill her water bottle at the sink. "Did I hear you talking about mucky paws? Why don't I like the sound of that?"

"Not 'mucky' – 'muddy'," Lexi insisted.

Lily swallowed hard. It had all sounded so

exciting out there in the paddock – the name, the logo, the T-shirts. But none of it could happen if her mum said no. "Muddy Paws – that's us."

As she screwed the top on to her water bottle, Jo gave her daughter a puzzled frown. "What do you mean – 'That's us'?"

"'No problem is too big or too small'," Lexi tried to explain. "We want to help people with their naughty pets."

"Where? When? How?"

Lily glanced at her dad for help but he was concentrating on his computer. It was down to her. "Mum, please let me and Lexi be Muddy Paws," she begged. "We won't bring any animals near the café and we'll make sure you don't have to do anything. We'll do it all by ourselves."

"We will," Lexi promised. She crossed

her fingers and tried again. "Please, Aunty Jo, please!"

* * *

Jo had gone out for her run without giving an answer. "I don't know yet. Don't rush me," were her parting words.

Lexi had kept her fingers crossed and Lily had sat down beside Alfie on the sofa. *Please say yes, Mum!* she said to herself over and over.

"How long will Aunty Jo be?" Lexi asked Matt as she paced up and down.

"About an hour – just enough time to tidy your room if you really want to get into her good books."

Without a word of protest, Lexi shot upstairs and tidied up like a whirlwind. Pyjamas folded and placed under pillow. Socks, knickers and T-shirts in drawers, shoes in a neat row under the bed.

"What do you think, Alfie? Will Mum say yes?" Lily stayed downstairs on the sofa. Then, as soon as her dad had finished on his computer, she took his place and googled "Top Tips for Dog Owners".

"Dogs are playful," she read on a new site and made notes. "They enjoy playing with toys, people and other dogs . . . Never shout at or punish your dog . . ."

She sat at the kitchen window, jotting down facts that she would use on the problem pets that owners would hopefully bring to Muddy Paws. If . . . if . . . if only . . .

When she heard the click of the latch on the garden gate, she looked up. "Quick, Lexi, come down!" she cried. "Mum's back!"

* * *

"And you promise to stay in the paddock and never to let any of these pets near the café?" Jo checked, looking rosy and windswept from her run.

"We promise!" Lexi and Lily chorused.

"And you'll do it all by yourselves?"

"Totally. You won't need to do a thing."

"You'll start with Madcap?"

"Yes!"

"And you actually believe you can get him ready for the Mellingham Show?"

"We do!"

Jo looked at the girls' faces, shiny with hope and excitement. She smiled back. "Then I give in. You win."

Out in the garden replanting the flower bed, Matt heard the verdict and poked his head through the open window. "Good for you," he told Lily and Lexi. "And good luck with Muddy Paws!"

* * *

"First, we design our logo." Early the next morning, Lily read from yet another list she'd made.

Lexi got out paper and felt-tips. "It has to be a doggy paw print," she decided and she started to draw. "How does that look?"

"Hmm." Lily thought the drawing looked more like a messy splodge than an actual animal paw.

"No good?" Lexi frowned and tried once more. "How about this?"

"Hmm," Lily said again. "Wait, I've got a better idea."

She went out into the garden and used a trowel to scoop earth into a dish. Then she came back into the kitchen and added some water. She stirred the dry earth and water together to make mud. "Alfie, come!" she called.

Alfie jumped down from the sofa and came to sniff at the dish. He turned away, disappointed.

"No, come back. I just want you to give me your paw and let me put it gently into this mud – see?" Lily smeared mud on to Alfie's right front paw. "Now Lexi has to bring us a piece of paper and you have to press your paw on to it – nice and firm, like that!"

Alfie wagged his tail and did as he was told. He made a perfect muddy paw print on the white paper.

"Duh-dah!" Lily exclaimed. "Now we give it to Dad and ask him to design some lettering."

"Cool," Lexi grinned. "'Muddy Paws' over the top and 'No problem is too big or too small' underneath."

"Then all we have to do is get Dad to photocopy it and take it to the shop in Mellingham that prints designs on T-shirts." Lily patted Alfie and thanked him. She was pleased with their work so far.

* * *

"Second, we print out some Muddy Paws leaflets and post them through letterboxes on the Green." Lexi was really into the task. "We tell everyone that we can train their problem pets."

"Third, we go into the paddock and check the hedges to make sure there are no gaps for pets to wriggle through and run away." Lily said this was really important.

"Fourth, we start to design our Muddy Paws website." Lexi was the one with big ideas. "It'll be where we give our top tips and run question and answer sessions."

"I'll help you with that," Lily's dad offered as he checked his emails.

"But now, we go and fetch Madcap." Down-to-earth Lily looked at her watch and saw that it was time for his next lesson. "Come on, let's go."

* * *

"Now, Madcap, we have to be strict," Lily told the mischievous pup at the start of their second training session. She held him up in the air, white paws dangling, and looked him in the eye. "It says so on all the websites."

"You have to learn who's boss," Lexi explained. "Doesn't he, Alfie?"

Her own pup sat quietly to heel, looking up at Madcap with his head to one side. *I'll believe it when I see it.*

"Stop it, Madcap. There's no point you looking cute and trying to lick my face," Lily protested.

Lexi agreed. "Today you're going to learn how to sit."

"But first we let you two play." Setting Madcap down on the grass, Lily took a ball from her pocket and threw it across the paddock. She and Lexi watched Alfie and Madcap chase after it, laughing when Madcap got there first. In his hurry to pick it up, he tripped over himself and did a forward roll. Quickly Alfie darted in and snaffled the ball.

"Good dogs!" Lexi called. "Fetch it, Alfie. Fetch!"

"How clever are you?" Lily cried when he came scampering back.

Lexi took the ball from Alfie and threw it again. This time Madcap got there first and brought it back.

"Good dog, Madcap!" the girls cried.

"We let them play until they get tired," Lily explained. "Then Madcap will need to sit down for a rest. That's when we teach him the sit command."

"Good plan," Lexi agreed.

The only problem was, Madcap never seemed to tire. Lily and Lexi lost count of the times they threw the ball and still he went racing after it with Alfie and the two of them came charging back. Then he would jump up and down and run round in circles until the girls threw it again.

"I'm hot!" Lexi sighed.

"My arm aches." What looked easy when it was written down was definitely hard work when you tried to do it.

Yip-yap, yip-yap!

"I don't care if he's tired or not, let's try with the treat," Lexi suggested.

So Lily took a small biscuit from her pocket and carefully held it in front of Madcap's nose, the same as before. "Sit!" she said sternly, then slowly she moved the treat up and over his head. "Sit, Madcap!"

Lexi held her breath and watched.

He tilted his head back and, almost without noticing, squatted down on his haunches.

"He's sitting, he did it!" Lexi cried.

"Good boy, well done." Lily grinned and popped the biscuit into his mouth.

"Alfie, it worked," Lexi sighed, sinking to her knees and cuddling him. "Did you see that? At last – Madcap learned to sit!"

Chapter Five

For a whole hour Lexi and Lily worked with Madcap on the "sit" command. They rewarded him with biscuits, praise and cuddles. Little Madcap lapped them all up.

Then, at two o'clock, Lily received a text message from Luke.

HEY, HOW'S IT GOING?

GOOD, she replied, before adding, HOW'S THE NEW ALBUM?

NIGHTMARE, he texted back. SO HOW SOON CAN YOU START AGILITY STUFF?

SOON, Lily promised.

By three the girls had taught Madcap not to jump up.

"Down!" Lexi would tell him in her stern voice. Then she would turn away until at last he stopped jumping and Lily moved in to reward him with pats and cuddles. "No more biscuits," she would tell him. "If we give you too many, you'll get fat."

Madcap squirmed and wriggled, then escaped to play with Alfie. Together they romped through the buttercups.

HEY, HOW'S IT GOING NOW? Luke texted at four o'clock.

MADCAP CAN SIT AND STAY DOWN, Lily replied. HE'S MADE FRIENDS WITH ALFIE.

COOL, Luke texted. YOU'RE SURE HE'LL BE READY FOR MELLINGHAM?

WE HOPE. Lily couldn't promise – she had to tell Luke the truth.

48

COOLIO. I TRUST YOU – I KNOW U CAN DO IT! ☺

"Look, Luke sent us a smiley face!" Lily sighed as she showed Lexi the message.

Lexi grinned as she sat on the grass in between Alfie and Madcap. She spoke sternly to the pups. "Tell him, Alfie. Say, 'Madcap, if you want to do well at the show, you'll have to work very, very hard!'"

* * *

"So we took Madcap home and Mrs Walker told us that Luke will be working in the studio until the day before the Mellingham Show," Lexi told her dad that night.

He was calling from America where he was working on a new idea for a reality TV show. Every evening he checked in to see how Lexi was getting on at her Uncle Matt and Aunty Jo's house.

Lexi was eager to fill him in on everything

that had been happening at Sea View. "So it's all down to us. It's OK, though. We've got a week and a half and Madcap's a fast learner."

"Tell him about Muddy Paws!" Lily hissed. Her dad had just brought home the T-shirts – white with a rainbow-coloured paw print and red lettering above and below. She put hers on straightaway.

"Oh and yeah, we've started a school for naughty pets," Lexi explained. "We called it Muddy Paws. Madcap's our first customer."

"Client," Lily corrected. She felt this was the right word.

Looking down at Alfie, she began to wonder if it would be possible to make a doggy T-shirt especially for him. "With the logo on the back," she whispered. "Because it if was on the front it would be under your tummy and no one would see it."

"So anyway." Lexi finished off the daily call with her TV executive dad. "Have to go now, Dad. Love you – bye!"

* * *

"It's amazing what you can do with a pair of scissors and some Velcro." That evening, after her run, Jo looked at Alfie with an amused smile.

The girls had taken one of their spare T-shirts, measured and then cut it, stitched it back together and made it so that it would fasten under Alfie's tummy. Now he too a the proud wearer of the Muddy Paws uniform.

"Here's one for you, Aunty Jo." Lexi handed her an adult-sized T-shirt. "Uncle Matt's already wearing his."

"Where is he now?" Jo asked.

Matt came into the sitting room with a bundle of Muddy Paws leaflets. "Hot off the printer," he exclaimed. "Ready to hand out."

So Jo took some for the café and the girls went around the village with Alfie, posting them through letterboxes. When they got back home it was time for bed, but at the top of the stairs Lily paused. "Lexi . . ." she began.

Lexi yawned. "What?"

"I was just thinking . . ."

"What?" Lexi yawned again.

"Luke's definitely in a big rush for us to get Madcap ready for Mellingham."

"So what?" Lexi asked. "I'm sure we can do it."

Lily's voice took on a troubled tone. "But the agility stuff isn't going to be easy." Just then her phone buzzed. "Hang on – it looks like a new message from Luke."

CAN'T WAIT 4 MCAP TO START JUMPING FENCES, she read. ☺ TXT ME WHEN IT HAPPENS.

Lexi snatched the phone. WILL DO, she replied.

Lily sighed then picked up where she'd left off. "So all I'm saying is – we have to get a move on."

Lexi agreed. "Tomorrow we'll teach Madcap to walk to heel."

"And the day after that we start with the fences," Lily decided.

* * *

"So cute!" Customers cooed over Alfie and his doggy T-shirt as they crossed the car park and went into the café the next morning. They picked up leaflets and read about Muddy Paws.

Lexi and Lily had just collected Madcap from Beech House and, with Alfie, they were teaching him to walk nicely on the lead.

"You keep him on your left-hand side and hold the lead in your right." As they crossed the lawn and reached the paddock, it was Lexi's turn to read out from the list of top ten tips. "Remember, Lily, you're the boss. Every time he pulls, you stand still."

Lily followed Lexi's instructions but it was hard – Madcap hated the lead. He just wanted to run around and play.

"Come on, Alfie, let's show him." Lexi put her pup on the lead. "Heel!" she said.

One ear pricked, the other flopping over his eye (the one with the brown patch), Alfie trotted nicely to heel. "Good boy!" Lexi smiled and patted him.

"That's how you do it," Lily told Madcap.

"No pulling, no messing about." The next time Madcap tried to run ahead, she stopped again. The puppy jerked the lead then halted, let the lead go slack and turned his head. *What's up?*

"Good," Lily said. "Now come back to me. That's a good boy. Heel!"

* * *

"Sit! Down! Come! Heel!" At the end of day two Lexi counted off the commands Madcap had learned, then she texted Luke.

MCAP DOING REALLY WELL.

COOLIO AGAIN ☺ BUT CAN HE JUMP YET? Luke texted back.

"No pressure!" Lily joked as she flopped down in the paddock beside Lexi. Together they watched Madcap and Alfie play.

For a while all they could see of the pups were the tips of two tails swishing through the long grass – one white and pointed, the other black and bushy. Soon Alfie came back while Madcap dashed on.

"Alfie really likes Madcap now that he's learning to be sensible," Lily said.

Don't speak too soon! Alfie gave Lily one of his looks.

"Oops!" Lexi saw Madcap's white tail vanish into the hedgerow overlooking the cliff path and then she heard a muffled yelp. "What's he done now?" she said as she scrambled to her feet and raced to rescue him.

Alfie ran with her.

"I hope he hasn't hurt himself." Lily caught up. Madcap might have found a way through the hedge and bolted along the edge of the cliff. She pictured the narrow path and the steep drop on to the rocks below.

"I can still hear him," Lexi muttered. "He can't have gone far."

With Alfie leading the way, they soon came to the stretch of hawthorn hedge which grew on top of a sandy bank. The bank was peppered with holes where rabbits had made their burrows.

Yip! Yip-yap! Madcap gave a muffled cry for help.

And there he was, with only his back end showing, pointy tail sticking straight up, body halfway down a rabbit-hole.

"Oh no – he's stuck!" Lexi cried.

Madcap wriggled and squirmed.

Alfie looked up at the girls. *OK, so what now?*

"Yeah, what do we do?" Lexi asked anxiously. What if Madcap was so stuck that they couldn't get him out? What if he ran

58

out of air and couldn't breathe?

"Start digging!" Lily said.

They scooped the sandy earth with their hands, making the entrance to the rabbit-hole bigger until at last Lily could reach in and pull Madcap out.

He blinked in the sunlight, shook his head and sneezed dirt from his nose.

"Poor thing!" Lexi murmured. "Was that scary?"

Madcap licked his teeth with his little pink tongue.

"Silly boy!" Lily cried, hugging him close. "No more running off."

"No more chasing rabbits."

"No more digging."

"No more getting stuck down holes!"

Chapter Six

Early the next morning, Lexi and Lily were about to set off as usual to collect Madcap from Luke's house on the Green.

"Whoo-hoo – Lily, Lexi!" Jo beckoned from the café doorway. "I've found your first customer for Muddy Paws."

"Client!" the girls chorused. They turned eagerly and ran back to the tea room where they found a woman in a blue cagoule and a shy girl of about six having breakfast at one of Jo's prettily laid out tables.

"Anyway, this is our second client," Lily

reminded her mum. "Madcap was our first."

"Meet Sian and her daughter, Annie," Jo said. "They're staying for a week at Lighthouse Cottages. They've been reading your leaflet."

"We have a problem pet," Sian told Lily and Lexi. "She's a chocolate Labrador called Venus."

"Where is she now?" Lily asked.

"We left her in the car. Shall we go and fetch her so you can take a quick look?"

Lily nodded while Lexi whispered into Alfie's ear. "Wow, our *second* client – that happened fast!"

"Can you ask your mum to put her on the lead and bring her into the paddock?" Lily said to Annie, who nodded then ran after her mother.

"So, this is Venus," Sian said, returning

after a couple of minutes. She led the Labrador into the paddock.

"What's the matter with her?" Lexi asked Annie, who hung back and still seemed shy. "Venus looks like a lovely dog."

Lovely and big and chocolatey, with a long, pink tongue and soft, velvety ears.

"You're gorgeous!" Lily whispered as she bent down to pat her.

Venus wagged her tail and waited for Sian to let her off the lead. "She's well trained in almost every way," the owner admitted. "She doesn't pull when she's on the lead and she always comes back when we call."

"We love her!" When Annie spoke for the first time, her voice was soft and there were tears in her eyes. "Before we came on holiday she never did a single thing wrong."

Sian agreed. "The problem is, since we

came to stay in Lighthouse Cottages, Venus has developed a very naughty habit."

The big Labrador seemed to know they were talking about her. She hung her head and looked up at Lexi and Lily with sorrowful eyes.

"So what does she do, exactly?" Lily prompted.

"Well, it started the day we arrived." Unzipping her rucksack, Sian pulled out a square of checked cloth. It was full of holes and frayed at the edges. "This is what she did to the landlady's brand-new tea towel."

"Venus chewed it?" Lexi asked.

"And this." With another sigh, their visitor pulled out a shredded cushion cover. "She tore the whole cushion to pieces on day two. There were feathers everywhere. Luckily I found an identical cushion in a shop in

Mellingham, so I was able to replace it. But look what she did to Annie's shoe."

There was a pause as Sian delved into the bottom of her rucksack and pulled out a sorry-looking trainer.

The shoe hardly looked like one. It had no laces and no tongue and there was a hole in the rubber sole where Venus had chewed right through.

Glancing at Venus, Lexi saw that her head had sunk so low that her chin touched the ground. She even ignored Alfie's invitation to get up and play.

Play! – that was the secret, Lexi realized. "Venus never chewed stuff before you came on holiday?" she checked with Annie.

"No. But Mum says if she goes on acting like this we'll have to go home early."

"So what's different at the cottages?" Lily wondered aloud.

Lexi looked thoughtful. "What does Venus play with while you're at home? Do you give her any toys?"

Annie nodded. "She's got a blue rubber bone with bells inside that jingle. It's her favourite."

"Did you bring it with you?"

"No, Mum forgot to pack it."

"And I bet you didn't bring any other toys." Sure that she'd found the key to the mystery, Lexi gave her verdict. "The problem is – Venus is bored!"

"Yes!" Straightaway Lily saw what Lexi was getting at. "Dogs love to play."

"Bored?" Sian echoed.

"That's why she's suddenly started chewing all the stuff she shouldn't," Lexi explained. "She's missing her favourite toy and she's bored because she has nothing to play with."

Venus still lay with her chin on the ground, looking up and sighing.

"Wait here." Lily was the first to act. She ran quickly back to the café and on into her mum's gift shop, where she found a wicker basket with a label that read "Dog Toys – £2.50". Rooting through it, she found what she was looking for – a hard rubber bone with jingling bells inside. She ran back, waving it in the air. "Guess what Mum sells in the Sea View Gift Shop!" she cried.

Sian smiled. "A toy bone – just like the one we have at home."

"But it's yellow," Annie said in her quiet, tearful voice.

"Venus won't mind what colour it is," Lily grinned. To prove it, she bent down and placed it under Venus's nose.

The chocolate Lab sniffed, then licked. She picked up the bone between her teeth and made it jingle. She let it drop then picked it up with her big front paws, let it go again then pounced, dropped it then ran around in circles, wagging her tail. Finally she looked up at Lily and gave the deepest bark the girls had ever heard. *Woo-oof!*

"Happy now?" Lexi asked Venus.

Woof! Jingle-jangle. A joyful Venus ran through the buttercups, all around the paddock with the toy clasped firmly between her teeth.

Chapter Seven

"How did today's training session with Madcap go?" Jo asked as the family gathered for supper. She'd started to show lots of interest in Muddy Paws since the girls' success with Venus earlier that day.

"Mega," Lexi replied. Alfie was snoozing in a warm corner of the kitchen.

"Madcap was really good," Lily added.

"Really and truly, we're not lying," Lexi insisted. "He played with Alfie, then we reminded him how to walk on the lead. He didn't pull or anything."

"So that's progress," Matt said. "And Alfie's a good role model."

"You hear that, Alfie?" Lexi called. "Uncle Matt says you're the best!"

Alfie opened one eye, gently wagged his tail then went back to sleep.

"Does Luke know that your hard work is beginning to pay off?" Jo asked.

Lily nodded. "We texted him. We're always asking how the new album's coming along, but he's only ever interested in Madcap."

Lexi picked up Lily's phone to read out Luke's latest message. "It just says this – 'Mellingham Show checked with me again – do we definitely want to enter Madcap into agility trials? I said yes'."

Jo's eyes opened wide. "Agility? That's training a dog to go over obstacles, isn't it?"

"Over jumps, through tunnels," Matt added. "Maybe Luke's expecting too much. Remember, there's only just over a week to go before the show."

"A week on Saturday," Jo reminded Lily. "Don't you think your dad's got a point?"

Lily gave an uneasy frown. "Maybe," she muttered.

"So we told Luke, no problem – Madcap will be ready," Lexi said. Ignoring the others, she hastily scooped a forkful of lasagne into her mouth.

* * *

"What did you mean – 'maybe'?" Lexi demanded after supper. It was bedtime and she'd followed Lily into her room. "We're *definitely* going to be ready for the show!"

Lily sighed and sat on her bed. "Are we? The agility tricks are really hard. I don't

71

know if Madcap has time to learn them."

Still Lexi refused to listen. "We're not going to let Luke down," she insisted.

"I don't want to – you know that. But what's worse – being honest and admitting that we can't do it, or letting Luke enter Madcap for something he's not really ready for?"

"We won't do either." Lexi always looked on the bright side but now she had to

convince Lily too. "We'll work really hard with Madcap. You've seen how quickly he learns stuff. I'm *sure* we can be ready."

"Oh, Lexi, I hope you're right," Lily sighed as she reached under her pillow for her pyjamas.

"Does that mean you'll keep on trying?" Lexi asked, fingers secretly crossed.

Slowly Lily nodded. "Yes," she agreed. "So you have to be up early and help me build an agility course – OK?"

* * *

"OK, I'm up! What do we do now?" Lexi asked, following Lily out of the house before breakfast next morning.

Lily had already thought it through. "We need hurdles and weaving poles, plus a collapsible tunnel and a hoop."

"How do you *know* all this stuff?" Though

she was up early, Lexi was still only half awake. Even Alfie had stopped in the house for a sleep-in. "Don't tell me – you looked on a website."

Lily grinned and nodded. "I thought we could make hurdles out of poles and support thingies they use for horses."

"So where do we get those from? Do we go all around the village asking to borrow them from a horsey person?"

"No. Follow me." Lily led the way to a big run-down stable in the corner of the paddock. The door was overgrown with brambles which Lily had to drag to one side. "Watch you don't get scratched, and mind the cobwebs."

It was musty and so dark inside that at first Lexi couldn't see what she was supposed to be looking at.

"The people who owned Sea View before us had a pony," Lily explained. "When they moved out they took the pony with them but left all this stuff behind."

"Jumping poles?" Now Lexi could make out three or four striped poles propped in one corner. "What do we rest them on?"

"Here." Lily started to carry some heavy plastic supports out into the paddock. "And you see those white fence post thingies? We can use them for weaving poles."

* * *

"Where do we get a hoop?" Lexi asked.

They'd set up three jumps and pushed the plastic sticks into the ground. There was a row of twelve with a gap of half a metre between each one.

"We could make one out of an old tyre,"

75

Lily suggested. "Dad's got one in the garage. And some rope. All we need to do is tie the rope around the tyre and hang it from the branch of that tree at the far side of the paddock."

* * *

"Collapsible tunnel . . ." By nine o'clock they had jumps, weaving poles and a hoop, but now even Lily was stuck.

Lexi thought hard. "Remember that Thomas the Tank Engine play-tent you had when we were little? We used to play with it out in the garden."

Lily nodded. "I think Mum kept it. It's folded up in a box in the attic."

"There was a square bit at the back that was Thomas's coal truck, linked to a round bit with a funnel that was his engine. Well, we could use the round bit as the tunnel . . ."

Chapter Eight

"And now, Madcap, we're going to teach you to jump these jumps, weave in and out of these poles, leap through this hoop and sprint through this tunnel," Lily explained carefully.

"Just like that!" Lexi laughed.

The girls had built the obstacle course, then collected Madcap from the Green. Now they were proudly showing him round.

Madcap yipped and yapped, falling over himself in his hurry to check it out.

"Come!" Lexi called, beating her palms

against her legs. "Come, Madcap!"

And, wonder of wonders – he came!

"Now sit!"

Amazing – he sat!

"Now watch and learn from Alfie," Lily told him.

"So, listen." Lexi spoke seriously to her pup, who was wearing his Muddy Paws T-shirt. "We have to show Madcap how to jump these jumps and weave in and out of those poles. I'll go first and you follow me – OK?"

Off she set with the wind in her hair, hurdling like an Olympic athlete – one, two, three jumps, with Alfie close behind. When she came to the poles she wove in and out and didn't stop until they came to the end.

"Stay, Madcap!" Lily ordered as the little Jack Russell whined to join in.

"Let him watch Alfie again then he can have a go," Lexi decided as she trotted back to the start.

"Go, Alfie!" the girls cried. They cheered him over the hurdles and in and out of the poles. They clapped and hugged him when he ran back to join them.

Then it was Madcap's turn. Lily crouched down and spoke seriously. "This time you follow Alfie – get it? You do everything he does."

Yip!

"Ready, go!" Lexi told the dogs.

It was fun to watch first Alfie then Madcap leap over the jumps.

"Madcap's legs are so short!" Lily laughed. "But it's like they've got springs in them – *boing!*"

They held their breath as Alfie led the

way down the line of poles. Would Madcap follow or would he get bored and scamper off to chase rabbits?

Yip-yip! Madcap sprinted in and out of the poles. He darted after Alfie and overtook him on the race back to the start.

"Brilliant!" Lily said as she patted him and gave him a biscuit. "You're a star, Madcap!"

"And now we're ready to try the hoop," Lexi grinned.

* * *

"Madcap's already a star in our paddock," Lexi told Matt after their first session with the obstacles. "But soon he'll be an even bigger star at the Mellingham Show."

"In only eight days from now," Matt pointed out. "I still think you're rushing things."

"It's OK, Dad – we've worked out his training programme." Like Lexi, Lily was starting to believe that Luke's pup wouldn't let them down. She showed her dad the latest sent message on her phone. "This was my text to keep Luke up to date."

MCAP CAN JUMP! ☺ HE CAN WEAVE THRU POLES ☺

"He called us back – actually took time out from the studio and called us," Lexi beamed. "He told us, coolio! But he was busy so he had to go."

Just then Jo came into the kitchen. "I haven't got long – I slipped out of the café to give you a message," she told Lily and Lexi. "I took a call from Rick Hawkins. It was about his cat, Jasmine."

Another client – their third! Lexi's eyes lit up. "What did you tell him, Aunty Jo?"

"I explained that he'd have to call the house to get in touch with Muddy Paws."

"What was wrong with Jasmine?" Lily managed to ask before her mum rushed back to work.

"Something about weeing all over Rick's carpets," Jo said, then she was gone.

Lexi's face fell. Wee on the carpet – "Erggh, stinky!" she groaned.

But Lily said she just had time to read up about the problem before Mrs Walker delivered Madcap for his morning session. "'House-training your cat'," she read out loud. "'Make sure to provide a clean litter tray in a prom . . . promin . . .'"

"Prominent." Her dad helped her out. "It means you put the tray down where it can easily be seen."

"Then you slowly move it closer to the

back door of the house." Lexi read over Lily's shoulder. "In the end you put the tray right outside the door."

"It says the cat won't even realize that he's doing his business outside. The problem is solved without him noticing." Lily logged off, happy that they had a plan for Jasmine. Muddy Paws would be ready for action as soon as their neighbour, Rick Hawkins, called.

"No problem too big or too small," Matt grinned, pointing at Mrs Walker, who was carrying Madcap towards the house.

"Too stinky or too dirty," Lexi added.

"Too crazy or too silly," Lily said, opening the door with a smile.

Chapter Nine

"No, Madcap – not like that!" Lexi wailed.

Lily watched the pup try to jump over the tunnel they'd made from the Thomas play-tent. He sprang high in the air, landed with a belly-flop on the roof of the tunnel, then slid back down to the ground.

"Watch Alfie. He'll show you how to do it," Lexi told him.

Alfie waited for the signal at one end of the tunnel. When Lily raised one hand and brought it down sharply, he sprang forward and ran swiftly through.

Lexi clapped her hands as he dashed clear. "Good job, Alfie. Well done! Now, Madcap – try again."

Lexi caught the pup and set him down at the entrance. She held him back, waiting for Lily to give the signal, then she let him go.

Grrr-grr! Madcap growled, then seized the rim of the tunnel between his teeth. He shook it to and fro.

"No, no, no!" Lexi sighed. "You're not supposed to wreck our tunnel, Madcap – you're supposed to run right through it!"

"I'll show him," Lily offered. Everything else had failed so she might as well try to make him copy her. Lexi grabbed hold of Madcap again while Lily went down on her hands and knees. She crawled into the tunnel.

"Uh-oh!" Lexi cried. "Come back,

Madcap! Lily, he escaped!"

Yip-yap-yip! A furry white face with floppy brown ears and shiny black nose appeared at the far end of the tunnel. Madcap bounded in to meet Lily. He covered her face in soft, wet licks.

"Not like that – that's the way out!" Lily cried from inside the tunnel. "No, stop, Madcap, that tickles!"

Lexi watched the tunnel tremble and shake. She saw Lily's feet trying to back out. She heard Madcap's happy bark.

"Stop – ouch – oh!" Lily cried.

Finally Lexi and Alfie dived in to help. Lexi grabbed Lily's feet and tugged, but somehow she herself was dragged into the tunnel. Alfie ran round to the exit and dashed inside to join Madcap. Soon all four had disappeared from sight. The tunnel shook, the dogs barked, the girls wrestled and giggled.

"Coaching Madcap isn't as simple and straightforward as you might hope," Matt told Mrs Walker as they stood watching the antics from the Sea View lawn. "In fact, next time you talk to Luke I'd warn him not to get his hopes up too high for the Mellingham Show."

* * *

Through Sunday, Monday and Tuesday of their second week of training Madcap, Lexi and Lily worked hard.

MCAP DOING WELL OVER HURDLES ☺, Lexi texted Luke on the Monday.

LIKEWISE THRU POLES ☺, Lily reported on Tuesday.

STILL NOT 2 HAPPY WITH TUNNEL ☹, Lexi admitted on Wednesday.

I KNOW U CAN DO IT!!! Luke texted back. STILL MEGA BUSY IN STUDIO. C U FRI NITE xxx.

"Three kisses!" Lexi sighed and looked forward to getting the signed T-shirts and albums that Luke had promised.

* * *

Meanwhile, on Tuesday at teatime, Rick Hawkins arrived at Muddy Paws with a carrier containing Jasmine, his young black and white cat. "I'm at my wits' end," he admitted. "I don't know much about cats because I haven't had one before. I inherited Jasmine when my sister went to work abroad. She said Jazzy was house-trained but it turns out she wasn't. Now my whole house stinks of cat pee."

"Don't worry – we can help," Lexi promised.

"I like Jasmine – don't get me wrong,"

Rick explained. "She's a friendly little thing, but I just can't stand the smell!"

Lily got down to business. "Why don't you bring her out to the paddock? We've already cleared a space in the stable and got a litter tray ready so we can show you what to do."

Following Lily and Lexi into the stable

and waiting for them to shut the door, Rick then opened the cat carrier and let Jasmine out.

"Cats don't like moving house," Lexi told him. "They get confused and scared. That's most likely why she's started to pee on your carpets."

"So you'll have to start training her to use a tray all over again." Lily showed Rick the tray lined with newspaper and he watched her pour the cat litter into it. Then she stepped back and let Jasmine take a sniff.

"Look – she definitely knows what it's for," Lexi said, watching the nervous cat step into the tray.

Jasmine scratched at the litter, then raised her tail and squatted. When she'd finished her pee, she scratched again and stepped daintily out of the tray.

"See, she's happy now!" Lily smiled. "But you have to keep the litter tray clean. You start with it in one place – say a corner of the kitchen – then you slowly move it towards the door."

"And in the end you can move it outside," Lexi added. "After that, Jazzy will find her own places in the garden to pee and poo."

"Got you," Rick nodded. "Thanks, Lily. Thanks, Lexi. That sounds like a good plan."

"No more smelly carpets," Lexi promised as they watched him put Jasmine back inside the carrier. Then they showed him out of the shed and back across the paddock, before waving him and Jasmine goodbye.

"Satisfied client number two. Muddy Paws is definitely up and running," Jo said when they went back to the house. "Good job, girls – I'm proud of you."

* * *

It was Wednesday evening when Lexi finally made some special Alfie time. She took him out on to the lawn, took off his Muddy Paws T-shirt and red collar, then brushed him from head to toe until his white and black coat shone. "You're so beautiful," she told him, landing a big kiss on the top of his head.

Alfie lapped up the attention. As Lexi packed away her brush and comb, he pushed his nose against her hand.

"No more stroking," she warned with a laugh. "We still have work to do. Come on, let's go to the paddock and set up some jumps for Madcap for tomorrow."

But Alfie and Lexi found that Lily had beaten them to it. There she was, already balancing striped poles on their supports.

Full of beans after his pampering session,

Alfie ran through the gate and soared over the first three jumps.

"Whoa!" Lily cried as he rushed by. "Hey, that was actually pretty cool!"

"He's good, isn't he?" Lexi murmured. She watched Alfie cut across the paddock and sail straight through the tyre hanging from the tree. "You know something – I bet Alfie would do really well in the agility trials."

"Not better than Madcap, though." Lily stayed loyal to Luke's pup. "After all our work, he'll be the best-trained dog in his section."

"But Alfie's amazing." Lexi watched him speed through the tunnel and race back to her. "Why didn't I think of this before?"

"You're saying we should enter them *both* into the competition – Alfie and Madcap together?"

Lexi smiled and nodded.

Lily thought it through. "But you know what that would mean?"

"Yeah, he might win a prize," Lexi said as she patted Alfie's head.

"No – duh!" Lily spelled it out. "They'd be in the same section. Alfie would be going up against Madcap, head to head."

"Ah!" Lexi said and she stopped to think. "But that wouldn't be a problem. In fact, it'd be cool. Come on, Lily – let's give Alfie a chance to be the star."

Chapter Ten

That night Lily lay awake thinking things through. She felt torn – on the one hand she'd love to see Alfie do well on Saturday, but on the other she really wanted Madcap to win.

Lexi didn't sleep well either. She realized Lily wasn't happy with her latest idea and she could see her point. After all, Muddy Paws was meant to be training Madcap, not getting sidetracked with Alfie.

"Forget what I said yesterday," Lexi suggested as she and Lily had breakfast next

morning. "I didn't stop to think."

"No," Lily disagreed. "It was me – I was wrong. Alfie's shown Madcap what to do. It's only fair he gets a chance to enter as well."

Slowly Lexi's eyes lit up. "Are you sure?"

Lily nodded. "Definite."

"Cool, Lily. Come on, Alfie. Let's go and collect Madcap and take them both for a walk on the beach!"

* * *

The tide was going out and the sun was high overhead when the girls ran down the wooden steps on to the wet beach. Small streams of clear water ran down towards the sea.

Madcap and Alfie ran and splashed, barked and ran again.

"They both love the beach," Lily sighed.

"Me too." Lexi was kneeling in the sand, making a sandcastle with her bare hands then laughing when the pups scampered up and knocked it down. They darted off again, running towards the streams of water still draining into the sea. "Hey, did you see that?" she said when first Alfie and then Madcap jumped clean over a narrow stream.

"They just did their first water jump!" Lily realized. "We started with hurdles, then weaving poles, hoop, tunnel (sort of), and now the water jump." She listed the obstacles that the pups could tackle. "Let's ask them to do it again – here where it's wider. I stand on this side with Alfie and Madcap. You stand at the other side. You say 'Come!'"

Lexi paddled across the stream and waited

for the pups to be ready. "Come, Alfie. Come, Madcap!" she called.

The puppies knew what they had to do and they wanted to do it but the new gap was too wide and their little legs just weren't long enough. Both Alfie and Madcap landed – *splash!* – in the stream.

"Oops!" Lily said.

The pups were dripping wet. They shook out their coats to dry.

Lexi and Lily both got cold showers.

"Hey!" Lexi cried.

"Hmm," Lily frowned. "Next time I think we should give them a running start."

* * *

"Only one more day." Lexi sat on the cliff path with Alfie and Lily to watch the sun set.

Since teaching the pups how to clear a water jump earlier that day, they'd made

two more Muddy Paws appointments for owners with problem pets – Ernie the hamster and Florence the rabbit. Then they'd fitted in a last-but-one session in the paddock with Madcap and Alfie.

"They've worked really hard," Lily said. "Let's cross our fingers for Saturday."

"What can go wrong now?" Lexi asked as Lily noticed a new text on her phone.

Everything was cool – they'd sent in the late entry for Alfie and heard from Luke's mum that their pop hero was still due home late on Friday afternoon, as planned. "I hope Luke remembers the signed T-shirts," she said to Lily.

"This message is from Luke," Lily muttered. Then she groaned and showed Lexi the text.

BAD NEWS, ☹☹☹, Lexi read. MANAGER WANTS US TO DO MORE RECORDINGS. HAVE TO WORK IN LONDON THIS WEEKEND.

WHAT ABOUT THE MELLINGHAM SHOW? Lexi texted back.

DON'T THINK I'LL MAKE IT AFTER ALL – SORRY, GIRLS.

Lily read the message and groaned. Lexi closed her eyes and felt the disappointment sink in. Alfie whined. Without saying a word the girls stood up, turned their backs on the setting sun and trailed back home to Sea View.

Chapter Eleven

"It won't be the same without Luke," Lexi told Jo and Matt sadly.

Back at base at Sea View, she and Lily had shared Luke's latest news.

"It's a pity, but things don't always work out the way we want them to," Jo said, while Matt sat at his computer, hard at work putting finishing touches to the design for a Muddy Paws website.

"What colour background would you like?" he asked Lily. "Blue or yellow?"

"Yellow, and can we make the pictures

move?" Lily asked.

"Luckily it was too late for the show organizers to put Luke's name on the posters," Jo reminded Lexi. "So most people weren't actually expecting him to be there."

"No, but *we* were," Lexi sighed. "We took Madcap home after we walked him on the beach and explained what had happened to Mrs Walker but she already knew Luke wouldn't make it. She said why don't Lily and I enter Madcap by ourselves? We're thinking about it."

"But you should." Jo wanted the girls' hard work with the little Jack Russell to pay off. "It would be shame for Madcap to miss out just because Luke can't be there."

Lexi nodded. "But I'm right, aren't I? It won't be the same."

* * *

"So?" It was Lily's turn to go into Lexi's room for one of their bedtime chats.

"What do we do?" Lexi sat cross-legged on her bed, hugging Mr Bobby, the floppy rabbit she'd had since she was two. "Do we enter Madcap without Luke or not?"

Lily sat beside her. "Funny – I came to ask you the same question."

"What did you expect me to say?" Lexi asked.

"I thought you'd say yes."

"You think we should?" For once Lexi couldn't decide.

Lily thought for a long time. "Yes," she said. "I do. I definitely think we should take Madcap to Mellingham whatever anyone says!"

* * *

"Today we do time trials." On Friday, their last day of training, Lily led the way. "See

105

this whistle, Alfie? You set off when I blow it and Lexi records your time on the stop-watch. Ready?"

She blew the whistle and Alfie set off over the hurdles, through the weaving poles, over the long jump they'd made with wooden planks from the shed and sand from the beach. Then he raced on through the hoop.

"One minute forty-five seconds . . .' Lexi kept track of his time. "Go, Alfie!"

He ran on, straight through the Thomas tunnel, then raced to the finish line, his feet hardly touching the ground.

"One minute and fifty-nine seconds!" Lexi went down on her knees and threw both arms around his neck.

"OK – ready, Madcap?" Lily held the whistle to her lips. "See if you can do it in one minute fifty."

Madcap sat at the start line, cute as anything with his head cocked to one side.

Lily blew and he bounded towards the hurdles – up and over, one, two, three, four times. Through the poles, over the long jump and through the hoop.

"One minute forty seconds!" Lexi cried.

Yip! Madcap darted towards the tunnel and disappeared.

Lily held her breath.

He flew out of the tunnel and sprinted for the finish.

"He did it! One minute fifty-two seconds!"

Yip! Madcap sprang into Lily's waiting arms.

* * *

"Maybe Luke will still make it." It was Saturday morning – the day of the Mellingham Show. Lexi sat staring out of the kitchen window with Alfie.

She and Lily had had no new word from London but they were still dead set on entering Madcap into the trials themselves. They'd even measured him for a Muddy Paws T-shirt and made one specially for him. Now they were due to collect him from Beech House at ten o'clock, then drive to Mellingham with Lily's dad. Jo would stay and look after the café as usual.

"Alfie, it's your big day!" Matt's bright voice cheered everyone up. "This is your chance to show who's top dog – you or Madcap."

Alfie wore his own T-shirt with pride. He woofed impatiently and went to the door. *Let's go!*

"It's OK – I know you went slow on purpose yesterday. You let Madcap win," Lexi whispered into his ear so that Lily couldn't hear.

He cocked his head and looked wise.

"Let's go," Lily said, breaking away from the computer at last. She led the way out to the car park, waving at her mum as they all got into the car.

Matt started the engine and looked at Alfie, Lily and Lexi in his overhead mirror. "Whatever happens today, you've done a great job with Madcap – all three of you."

"I just wish Luke could see it," Lexi frowned.

If . . . if only! Lily secretly crossed her fingers and stared out of the window.

* * *

Anyway, there was no time to think what might have been. Mrs Walker was waiting for Lexi and Lily at the front door of Beech House. "Here, take Madcap," she said hurriedly. "I have to be somewhere in ten minutes, but good luck, everyone. I hope Madcap behaves himself!"

Then it was time to dress Madcap up in his Muddy Paws uniform while Lily's dad drove on down the narrow country lanes, out on to a main road which took them all to Mellingham. Matt followed the signs to the Mellingham County Show and parked the car in a field marked out with orange tape. Then the girls put Alfie and Madcap on their leads to hurry past stalls selling horse tack, dog baskets and garden seats.

"Just in time." Matt breathed a sigh of relief as they reached the show ring and a voice came over the loudspeakers to announce the start of the agility trials.

"Section one for dogs under two years."

"Wow – huge course!" Lexi muttered to Lily as she caught sight of the obstacles laid out in the ring.

"Humungous crowd!" Lily whispered. There seemed to be thousands of people gathered to watch.

"There will be ten dogs in this section," the loudspeaker voice announced. "First to go is Peanut, a brown and white Border collie, with his owner William."

Lily and Lexi watched with Madcap and Alfie as Peanut cleared six hurdles and his owner urged him on.

"He's good," Matt said.

"You two are better," Lexi told Alfie and Madcap. "Don't listen to Uncle Matt."

The whole crowd went "ooh!" as Peanut wove through a set of poles. They clapped as he leaped through the hoop and sprinted through the tunnel. Then they cried "*aah!*" – Peanut had landed smack in the middle of the water jump.

"We have one wet dog," the announcer reported. "That's a ten-second penalty for Peanut, I'm afraid."

The crowd clapped anyway as the young Border collie completed the course in two minutes twenty-five seconds.

"And now," said a new voice on the

loudspeaker, "we interrupt the action in the main ring to tell you about some very special visitors to the Mellingham Show."

A white Range Rover crawled slowly towards the ring and all heads turned.

"Isn't that Mrs Walker's car?" Matt said while Lexi and Lily craned their necks to see.

Excited spectators crowded round the car and peered inside.

Lily's heart missed a beat. She held tightly to Madcap as the Range Rover drew near. Lexi stood on tiptoe with Alfie to get a better view. They saw the car stop and all four doors open about ten metres from where they stood. Not one but four familiar figures stepped out.

"Ladies and gentlemen, we're thrilled to welcome four young people whom you'll all recognize. Please say hello to Sammy, Jude, Luke and Ryan – in other words the world-famous boy band, Mellingham's very own Up Front!"

Chapter Twelve

"You made it!" Lexi and Lily beamed as Luke split off from the rest of the band and pushed his way towards them.

He nodded. "At the very last minute our manager gave us the day off. We came on the train and Mum picked us up from the station. Hey, cool T-shirts," he grinned, noticing Madcap and Alfie in their Muddy Paws outfits. "Which reminds me . . ."

The girls watched him unhitch a rucksack from his shoulder. He opened it and took out two Up Front T-shirts. "Signed by me,

Sammy, Jude and Ryan," he said as he handed one to Lexi and one to Lily. "You'll get the new album as soon as it's finished."

"Oh, cool!" Lexi held the T-shirt up against her.

"Thank you!" Lily grinned.

Smiling back, Luke took his puppy from Lily. "So, Madcap, did the Muddy Paws team train you well?"

Yip! Madcap squirmed and wriggled. He licked his owner's face with joy.

"He's been amazing!" Lily cried. "You wait and see."

"Your mum didn't tell us you were coming!" Lexi sighed as she slipped her new T-shirt into her bag.

"I guess she wanted it to be a surprise."

"Well, it was – for everyone." Lexi grinned from ear to ear.

In the distance, the crowd mobbed Ryan, Sammy and Jude. The Up Front boys were signing autographs and chatting, posing for photos and loving it all.

Meanwhile there was an announcement over the loudspeaker. "We're still waiting for Lexi to bring her dog Alfie into the show ring. Has anyone seen Lexi and Alfie from Muddy Paws?"

"Oops!" Lexi had been so excited that she'd missed the first announcement. "We're here!" she cried, pushing her way towards the entrance.

"Good luck!" Lily called above the noisy crowd. She stayed with Luke and Madcap, keeping her fingers crossed. "They look so small out there in the middle of the show ring," she whispered.

But Lexi wasn't nervous. She crouched beside Alfie, waiting for the starter's whistle. "Don't worry – I'll help you get round in a good time," she promised.

Alfie was bright-eyed and alert. The tip of his pink tongue showed between his front teeth. The second he heard the whistle he was off.

He cleared the hurdles, no problem, then sprinted between the poles with Lexi alongside. She pointed to the hoop and watched him sail clean through, then the tunnel – no problem.

"Water jump!" she yelled and pointed.

Alfie took off and ran like the wind. He cleared the water with half a metre to spare. "Long jump!" She was there waiting for him at the last obstacle as he pounded towards the sandpit and took off again.

"A wonderful clear round!" the voice on the loudspeaker announced. "In two minutes fifteen seconds. That puts Alfie from Muddy Paws in first place!"

The crowd cheered. Lexi hugged Alfie. Lily ran to meet them as they came out of the show ring and the next competitor went in.

"You were brilliant!" Lily jumped up and down for joy. "You're in the lead. How cool is that?"

"When is it our turn?" Luke had followed Lily to the edge of the ring and was watching anxiously as a dog called Pepsi knocked over the first hurdle. He had Madcap tucked under his arm and refused to sign autographs until the trials were over.

Lily read the list of entries. "Madcap's next. We're last to go in this section."

Luke swallowed hard. "Will you take him in for me?" he asked Lily. "You've done all the work with him and I wouldn't know where to begin."

But Lily shook her head. "He's your dog."

"Yes but . . ."

"People in the crowd want to see you, not me."

Still Luke pulled back. "I can't. My stomach's knotted up."

Lexi couldn't believe it. Wasn't this the pop idol who stood on a stage in front of thousands of screaming fans? Seeing Pepsi finish the course in two minutes fifty-eight seconds plus a time penalty, she gave Luke a little shove. "*Both* go!" she hissed. "You and Lily together – the judges won't mind!"

So that's what happened. Lily took Madcap from Luke and put him down on the ground. She and Luke followed him into the ring.

"And finally we have Madcap with Luke and Lily," the announcer said. "Madcap is our second contestant from Muddy Paws."

A huge cheer went up. In fact, the crowd went mad.

"Go, Luke! Go, Madcap! Go, Muddy Paws!"

"Ready?" Lily checked with Madcap.

He looked up at her with his cheekiest face then led Luke and Lily to the start line.

"Aah!" The crowd made it clear that they'd never seen anything so cute as this little Jack Russell showing his famous owner what to do. They burst into applause and almost drowned out the sound of the starter's whistle.

But Madcap heard it and shot off towards the hurdles. Lily and Luke ran with him, holding their breath as his springy little legs worked overtime. He was up and over six times without a pause and dodging in and out of the poles before they knew it. He was through the hoop and into the tunnel, out again and heading for the water jump.

Lily couldn't look – she closed her eyes and prayed. There was no splash. Madcap had cleared the water. Luke was already waiting by the long jump.

His legs are too little! Lily groaned to herself. And again she closed her eyes. When she opened them again, Madcap was crossing the finish line and springing up into Luke's arms.

"Madcap goes clear in . . ." There was a long pause while the announcer checked the stopwatch. "In two minutes fifteen seconds. Ladies and gentlemen, two dogs from Muddy Paws went clear in exactly the same time. It's a tie for first place between Alfie and Madcap!"

Madcap licked Luke then he licked Lily. He sprang out of Luke's arms and ran to meet Alfie who was sprinting into the arena ahead of Lexi. As the crowd cheered, the two happy winners greeted each other in the middle of the ring and rolled on the ground. They jumped up and rolled again until Lexi and Lily ran to grab them while Luke sprinted for cover into the judges' tent before the crowd closed in and totally mobbed him.

* * *

"*Two* red rosettes!" Lexi and Lily were bursting with pride.

They sat with Madcap and Alfie on the back seat of Mrs Walker's Range Rover while Luke sat in front with his mum. With their rosettes pinned to their collars and still wearing their Muddy Paws T-shirts, the two proud pups soaked up their owners' praise.

"First equal!" Luke shook his head in disbelief. "I don't know what to say!"

"How about thank you to Lily and Lexi?" Mrs Walker drove carefully down the lanes back to the village. "In less than two weeks they've taken Madcap to Muddy Paws and changed him from a puppy who wouldn't do a single thing he was told into a perfectly trained dog who wins prizes."

"Yeah, thanks," Luke told the girls. "You're amazing."

"It wasn't just us," Lily blushed. "Alfie did loads too."

"So thanks, Alfie."

Woof! Alfie said.

Yip! Madcap added.

Luke grinned. "And would you like to carry on working with my cute little guy when I'm away on tour?"

Lexi and Lily didn't wait a second to reply. "You bet!"

"He's so smart, if you teach him new tricks maybe we could get him a part in a movie or a TV commercial?" Luke thought of ways of turning Madcap into a superstar. "He could be the little dog that saves the guy's life when he's trapped inside a burning building. He could raise the alarm during a bank robbery . . ."

Yip! Madcap sounded eager but Alfie stayed silent on the back seat of the car. He gave Madcap a look that said, *Remember – without me, you're nothing!*

Lexi and Lily giggled and stroked them both.

"Oops, in fifteen minutes we're supposed to be back at Muddy Paws," Lily suddenly remembered "We have to see Ernie."

"The hamster with the weight problem," Lexi explained to Luke.

They were crossing the Green, still heading for Sea View. "Don't worry, we'll make it home just in time," Mrs Walker said.

"And after that it's Florence the rabbit who likes to dig holes," Lexi reminded Lily. "We have to find a way to stop her escaping from her run."

Smiling, the girls looked ahead to a busy evening for Muddy Paws.

And Alfie and Madcap sat on the back seat, their rosettes fluttering in the breeze.

Breezy is a shy foal whose mother has died.
Carefully, Lexi and Lily befriend her.
But just when they are making progress,
they learn Breezy might be taken away.
How can the girls convince Breezy's
owners to let her stay?

And there are lots of other wonderful
animals to meet in the second
Muddy Paws story . . .

Turn the page for a sneak preview

of the next book . . .

Making Friends
With Breezy

"Hubert needs to eat grass, hay and lettuce," Lily told the Simons twins.

The chubby black guinea pig sat glumly on Jon's lap in the old stable in the Sea View paddock.

"He *is* very fat," Lexi said. "What else do you give him?"

"Cornflakes," Sam admitted.

"And cake," Jon added.

"No more cake!" Lily knew they had to be strict. "But you can give him kiwi fruit. That's good for him."

"OK." It was time for the twins to leave. Jon put poor Hubert in his cage. "Your T-shirts are cool," he told Lily. "I like the logo."

She smiled and tugged at the hem of her T-shirt to straighten it so that the twins got a better view of the paw print design and rainbow letters which spelt out the name, Muddy Paws.

"Bring Hubert back next week," Lexi suggested. "We'll take another look at him then."

* * *

"So what's wrong with Dino?" Lexi asked Daisy Goodwin.

The pure white Persian cat was curled up inside his pet carrier, gazing out with enormous, sad green eyes.

Miss Goodwin patted her neat grey hair into place then sighed. "He's not himself. He lies in his basket all day long. Then when I have visitors, he slinks off and hides behind the curtains."

"Is he eating OK?" Lily wanted to know.

"Not really. He seems to have lost his appetite."

"Did you take him to the vet?" Lexi was anxious because Dino looked so sorry for himself.

"Yes. She told me she couldn't find anything wrong."

"Hmm." Lily thought hard. "We need to read up about this," she told Dino's worried owner.

"We'll find out what to do to make him feel better," Lexi assured her.

"I've tried everything I can think of," Miss Goodwin sighed, lifting Dino's carrier from the table. The sad, fluffy cat gave a little miaow.

"We'll do our best," Lily promised.

"We *definitely* will." Lexi planned to surf the net until they came up with an answer. "We'll call you as soon as we can."

* * *

"OK, Alfie – walkies!" After Miss Goodwin and Dino had gone, Lexi stood with Lily on the lawn at the back of the café and called her little dog.

Alfie bounded towards her, a happy bundle of white and black fur.

"Come on, Alfie. We just have time for a walk before the sun goes down." Lily led the way along the footpath towards the beach. Passing Lighthouse Cottages, they came to the side gate leading into the grounds of Dentwood Hall where they stopped to say hello to the three peacocks living there. The male bird puffed out his electric-blue chest and spread his beautiful tail feathers. He let out a high-pitched screech – "E-e-elp! E-e-elp!"

"Woof!" Alfie urged from further along the path.

"Hang on, Alfie – we're coming!" Lexi laughed.

Soon they came to the wooden steps leading down to the beach. Alfie scampered ahead.

"Wait for us," Lily begged. No way could the girls keep up.

He was still ahead of them, already splashing at the water's edge when Lexi and Lily rolled up their jeans and stepped on to the warm sand. The waves broke and curled on to the shore, the sea sparkled in the evening light.

"Alfie's found a friend." Lexi was the first to spot the golden retriever that lolloped up to little Alfie, tail wagging. "It looks like Molly from the Hall."

They raced to the shore then waded in to the foaming water to join the dogs.

"Brrr!" Lexi shivered.

"Watch out – here comes Monty!" Lily recognized the big chestnut horse that galloped towards them from the far end of the beach. His hooves thundered along the shoreline, kicking up wet sand.

"Hi, Mrs Finch!" Lexi waved as horse and rider drew near.

"Hello, girls." The owner of Dentwood Hall reined Monty back. She stopped for a quick chat. "It's a lovely evening."

Lily shaded her eyes with her hands. "Monty's so strong and fast," she sighed.

The chestnut horse breathed heavily after his gallop. His neck was arched and he pranced on the spot.

"He's lovely, isn't he?" Mrs Finch smiled down at the girls and the dogs. "You must visit him at the Hall. Perhaps you'd like to meet Phoebe, our Shetland pony, too."

"Wow!" Lexi gasped.

"Yes, please!" Lily jumped at the chance.

"Has either of you been around horses before?" Rosemary Finch asked as she tugged the peak of her hard hat further down her forehead.

Lexi and Lily shook their heads. Cats, dogs, hamsters, guinea pigs – yes. Horses – no.

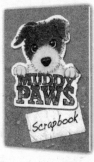

Find out what happens to Lexi and Lily in the next Muddy Paws adventure,
***Making Friends with Breezy,* and receive a FREE Muddy Paws scrapbook!**

The scrapbook is the ideal place for you to put pictures of all your favourite animals and pets. Plus there are activities perfect for all Muddy Paws fans!

To receive your Muddy Paws scrapbook, you need to collect two tokens. One is below and you'll find the second token in *Making Friends with Breezy*. Then simply fill in the form on this page and send it to us with both tokens and we'll send you your FREE Muddy Paws scrapbook!

Send one completed form and two tokens to: The Muddy Paws Scrapbook Offer, the Marketing Department, Hachette Children's Books, 338 Euston Road, London, NW1 3BH

Closing date: 31 January 2014

TERMS AND CONDITIONS

(1) Open to UK and Republic of Ireland residents only (2) You must provide the email address of a parent or guardian for your entry to be valid (3) Photocopied tokens are not accepted (4) The form must be completed fully for your entry to be valid (5) Scrapbooks are distributed on a first come, first served basis while stocks last (6) No part of the offer is exchangeable for cash or any other offer (7) Please allow 28 days for delivery (8) Your details will only be used for the purposes of fulfilling this offer and, if you choose [see tick box below], to receive email newsletters about other great Hachette Children's books, and will never be shared with any third party.

- ✂ -

Please complete using capital letters (UK Residents Only)

FIRST NAME:

SURNAME:

DATE OF BIRTH: DD MM YYYY

ADDRESS LINE 1:

ADDRESS LINE 2:

ADDRESS LINE 3:

POSTCODE:

PARENT OR GUARDIAN'S EMAIL:

I'm happy to receive email newsletters and information about other great
Hachette Children's books (I can unsubscribe at any time).

ONE TOKEN

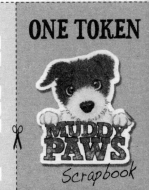

www.hachettechildrens.co.uk